Jake

For Jake . . . and Mark
who have made the book the way it is

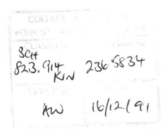
A Beaver Book
Published by Arrow Books Limited
20 Vauxhall Bridge Rd, London SW1V 2SA
An imprint of Century Hutchinson Ltd

London Melbourne Sydney Auckland
Johannesburg and agencies throughout the world

First published in 1988 by Hutchinson Children's Books
Beaver edition 1990

Set in Century Old Style by The Graphic Unit, London

Printed and bound in Great Britain
by Scotprint, Musselburgh, Scotland

ISBN 0 09 967480 7

Jake

Deborah King

BEAVER BOOKS

Early morning had never been Jake's favourite time of day. He preferred to wake up slowly and take things easy.

But today was different. Jake had a very good reason for getting up. Grandpa was coming, and they were going to the beach.

But when Jake looked downstairs, Grandpa wasn't there!

That's funny, thought Jake. I wonder if he's in the garden? But he couldn't find Grandpa anywhere.

'He's never been this late,' he whined. 'Surely he can't have forgotten me.'

Jake couldn't bear to wait a minute longer. The sun was shining and somehow he'd *got* to find Grandpa. He slipped quietly through the back door and was on his way.

At the end of the lane he met a party of schoolchildren running down to the beach.

I wonder if they've seen Grandpa, thought Jake.

But the children just wanted to play, and soon Jake was too busy with his head under water to think about Grandpa.

Dripping wet by now, and rather bedgraggled, Jake stumbled up the beach and bumped straight into some grown-ups.

They're *sure* to have seen Grandpa, he thought.

But for some reason they weren't at all helpful.

Jake was in trouble now.

All alone, and wishing he'd stayed in bed after all, Jake suddenly had an idea. 'Perhaps if I bark *really* loud Grandpa will hear me and come to my rescue.'

Everyone in the whole world heard him, everyone *except* Grandpa.

It was the windsurfers who set him free. 'Anything for a quiet life,' they told him. But Jake wasn't listening.

'I'll show them a trick or two,' he barked.

The windsurfers were soon bored with him. They picked up their
sailboards and headed down to the sea. Jake went too. Perhaps Grandpa
is taking his morning dip, he thought.

And before anyone could stop him, he was afloat!

'If I keep to the shallows,' he barked, 'Grandpa is bound to see me.'

He didn't notice the wind getting up. In no time at all it was blowing him further and further out to sea.

He was going very fast.

TOO FAST!

SPLASH!

But Jake was rescued just in time.

As he was rowed across the bay, he barked as loud as he could, just in case Grandpa could hear him.

WOOF!   WOOF!   WOOF!

A young man in a yacht recognised that bark only too well.

'Jake! What are you doing out here in the middle of the ocean?' he cried. 'And where's your old friend?' Jake wished he knew.

'Well, you won't find him where we're going,' continued the young man, hauling Jake aboard

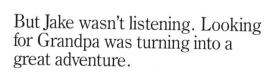

But Jake wasn't listening. Looking for Grandpa was turning into a great adventure.

Once ashore, Jake was so busy scrambling over cliffs and exploring the coves and rockpools that he almost forgot about Grandpa.

It was while he was lying in a pool that he suddenly remembered.

I suppose I'd better take a look,
he thought.

But he was gone too long and he missed the boat.

There was nothing for it but a long cold swim. As he paddled his way through the deep, murky water he came to the conclusion that looking for Grandpa hadn't been such a good idea after all.

It wasn't an easy ride home. The wind was blowing even harder and the boat rocked and rolled in the swell. 'No use calling for Grandpa now,' he sighed, and he hid down below. For once in his life he had nothing to say.

Not until he was safely ashore did Jake begin to feel like a real dog again.
'It's good to be back on dry land!' he barked.

But it just wasn't the same without Grandpa and, shaking the sand from his eyes, Jake thought of one last place where Grandpa might be . . .

. . . the village pub.

And he wasn't going to walk there, not if he could help it.

But even the barman hadn't seen Grandpa. No one had.
   Jake had finally run out of ideas. It was time to call off the search and head for home.

However, Jake was in for a surprise. Who should be waiting for him, but Grandpa!

'Where *have* you been all day?' exclaimed his old friend. 'Why didn't you wait for me this morning?'

All at once, Jake realised his mistake. And from that day on, he made up his mind never to get up too early, *ever* again . . .

. . . and he never did!

Other titles in the Beaver/Sparrow Picture Book series: